Hello there, says Chair.

HAVE a LOOK, says BOOK.

Richard Jackson & Kevin Hawkes

A Caitlyn Dlouhy Book
ATHENEUM BOOKS FOR YOUNG READERS
New York * London * Toronto * Sydney * New Delhi

atheneum

ATHENEUM BOOKS FOR YOUNG READERS • An imprint of Simon & Schuster Children's Publishing Division • 1230 Avenue of the Americas, New York, New York 10020 • Text copyright © 2016 by Richard Jackson • Illustrations copyright © 2016 by Kevin Hawkes • All rights reserved, including the right of reproduction in whole or in part in any form. • ATHENEUM BOOKS FOR YOUNG READERS is a registered trademark of Simon & Schuster, Inc. • Atheneum logo is a trademark of Simon & Schuster, Inc. For information about special discounts for bulk purchases, please contact Simon & Schuster Special Sales at 1-866-506-1949 or business@simonandschuster.com. • The Simon & Schuster Speakers Bureau can bring authors to your live event. For more information or to book an event, contact the Simon & Schuster Speakers Bureau at 1-866-248-3049 or visit our website at www.simonspeakers.com. • Book design by Ann Bobco • The text for this book is set in Big Caslon. • The illustrations for this book are rendered in gouache. • Manufactured in China • 0116 SCP • First Edition • 10 9 8 7 6 5 4 3 2 1 • Library of Congress Cataloging-in-Publication Data • Jackson, Richard, 1935– Have a look, says book. / Richard Jackson ; illustrated by Kevin Hawkes. — First edition. • pages cm • "A Caitlyn Dlouhy Book" • Summary: Through illustrations and simple, rhyming text, a book invites its reader to explore fluffy, furry, or squishy objects and creatures, both real and imaginary, that are found within its pages. • ISBN 978-1-4814-2105-8 (hardcover) • ISBN 978-1-4814-2106-5 (eBook) • [1. Stories in rhyme. 2. Books and reading—Fiction. 3. Touch—Fiction. 4. Textures—Fiction.] I. Hawkes, Kevin, illustrator. II. Title. • PZ8.3.J1357Hav 2016 • [E]—dc23   2014034953

With thanks to George Ella Lyon—
friend and inspiration—
whose many books have touched me.

And
to Peter Catalanotto—best father
—R. J.

To my father and mother, who love books
—K. H.

Yes a look,
says Book . . .

a look,
a listen,

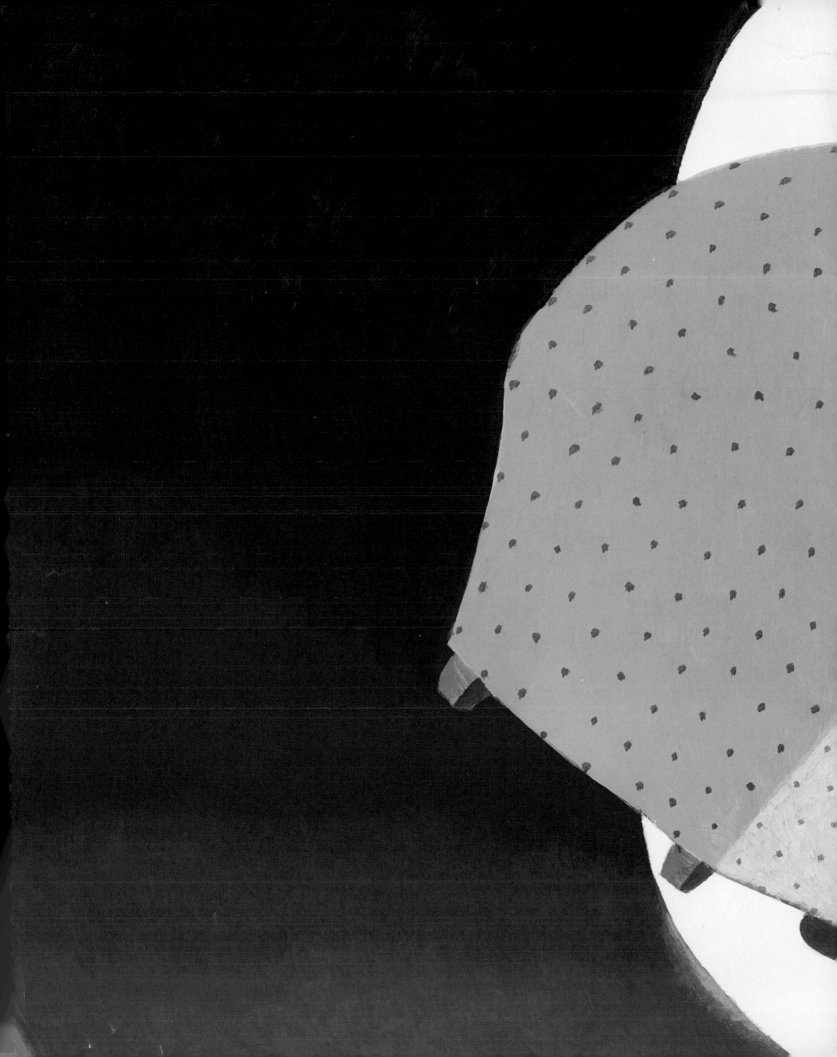

and
a
touch
as
such.

I am

furry

says Kitten.

I am W**oo**l**y** says Sock.

I am **Wet** says Mitten.

drip-
drip

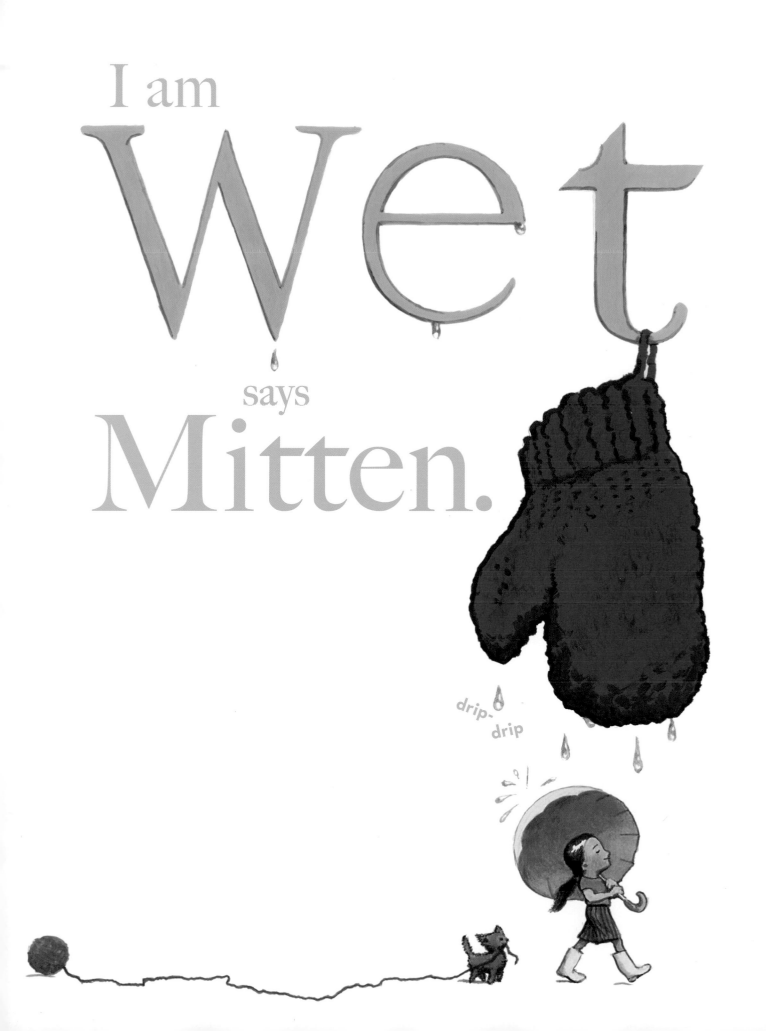

We are fleecy

says
Flock
(stock-still
on a rock).

I am **Shaggy** says

Llama.

I am

mossy says Trail.

I am 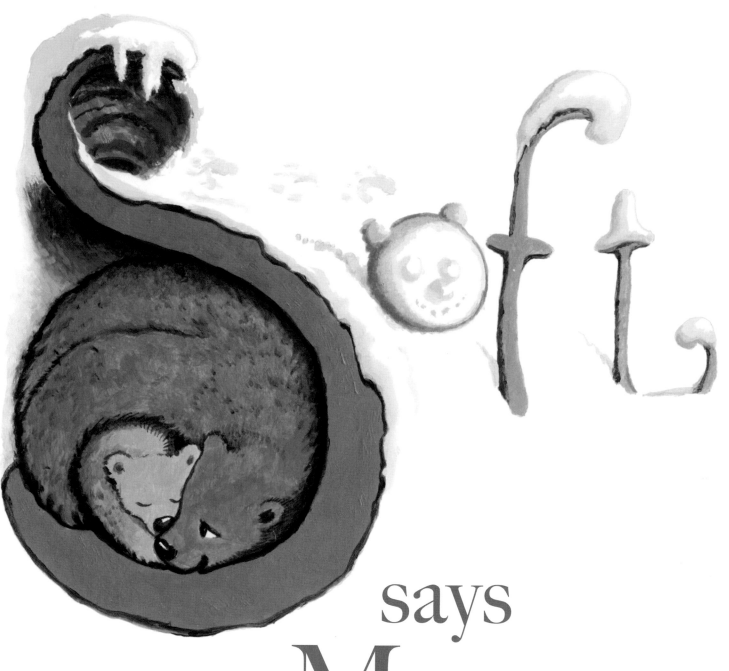oft,

says

Mama.

I am gluey

says
Snail

(with its tail
in a pail).

And look, look at me . . .

I am splashy

says

Whale.

I am Scratchy says Tutu.

I am toothy

says Comb.

I am

am

says

Igloo.

I am

Gnarly

says
Gnome
(at home on a dome).

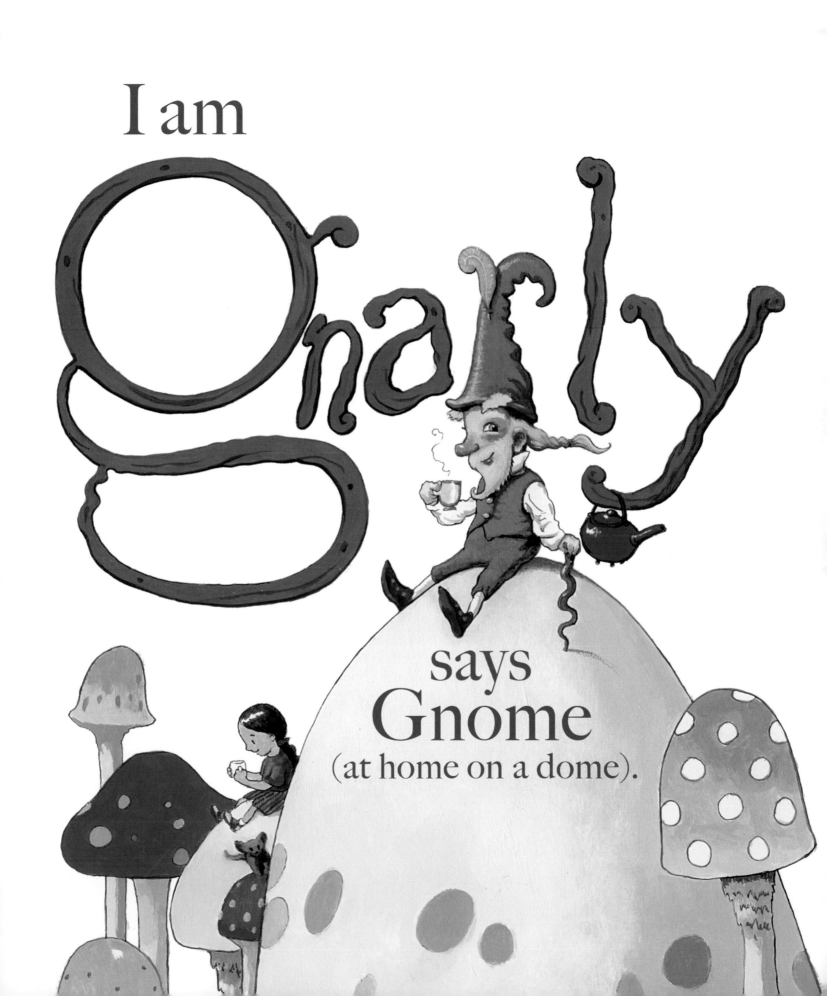

I am **fluffy**
says Feather.

We are **nubbly**
say Knees.

I am **dry**
says
Heather.

We are
barky
say Trees.

And we . . . why, we are

say
Peas.

(Now, eat these up, please!)

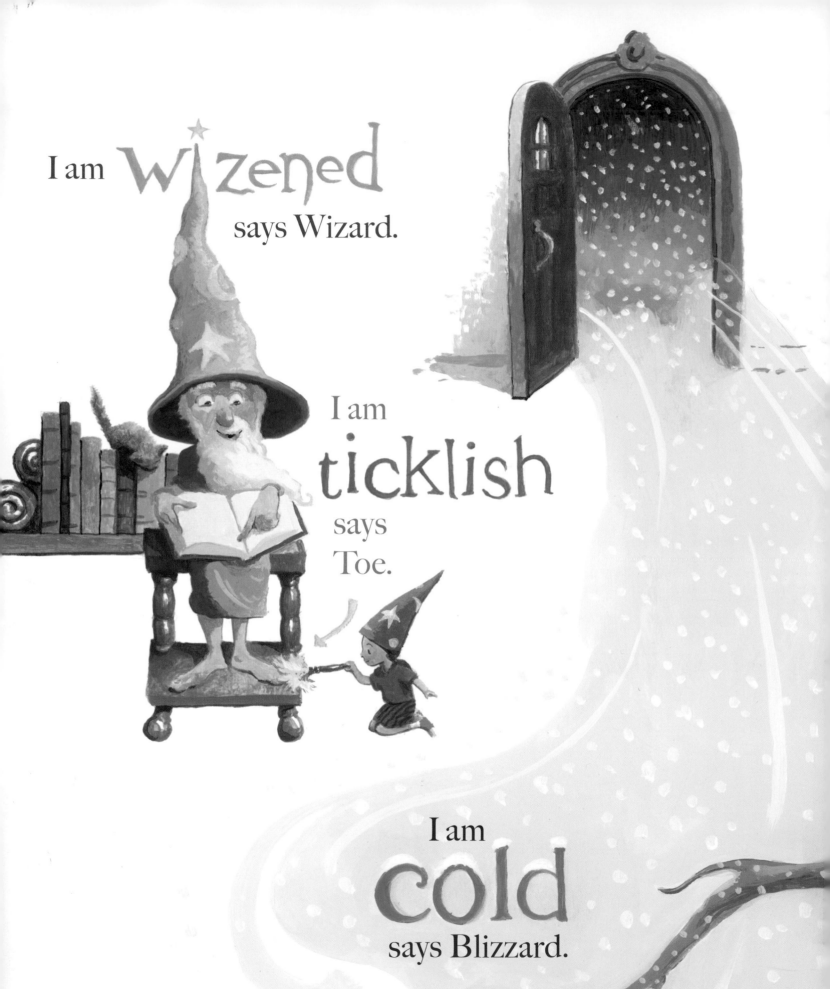

I am **WIZENED** says Wizard.

I am **ticklish** says Toe.

I am **cold** says Blizzard.

I am **Silky**

says Crow.

Caw!

Wheeeeeeee!

Whoa!

I am steamy says Loco.

Let's
take
a
break...

for a minute or so?

I am h⚬t

says Cocoa.

Oh, YUM.

I am **Crumbly** says Cake.

Oh,
YUM
even
more.

I am Cmfy

am

says Chair.

(Try not to spill
or get crumbs on the floor.)

I am cozy, says Papa.
How about you?

Comfy the one,
cozy the pair,
says the book in the nook:

Toodle-oo, you two there.

Thanks for the listen,

thanks for the touch,

thanks for the look,

thank you so much.